Dedicated to my sister, Aileen

Copyright © 1991
Mary Jane Flynn

Published by
Storytellers Ink
Seattle, Washington

ISBN 0-9623072-3-8

Printed in Mexico.

If a seahorse wore a saddle. . .

. . . would you tie him to a tree?

Would you keep him in your yard
for all your friends to come and see?

Would you use him as a chair
so you could eat and watch TV?

Would you hang your clothes
upon him?

Would you make him tie your shoes?

Would you send him out for pizza . . .

. . . and the early morning news?

When you played a game of checkers
would you always make him lose?

Would you wear a mask to scare him
in the middle of the night?

Would you take his favorite T-shirt
just to try to start a fight?

Would you tie a string around him
and then use him for a kite?

If you stopped to think
about it. . .

. . . you would know these things
are wrong.

And a seahorse treated this way
would go home before too long.

But this story isn't over,
and there's time before the end . . .

. . . to find out where he might take you
if the seahorse were your friend.

He might let you ride down with him
to the bottom of the sea. . .

That's where all the sunken pirate ships
and treasure chests must be!

He might take you to the castle
of an underwater king . . .

You might see a giant octopus . . .

. . . or hear a mermaid sing.

You'd see fish of every color,
shape and size
all swimming by . . .

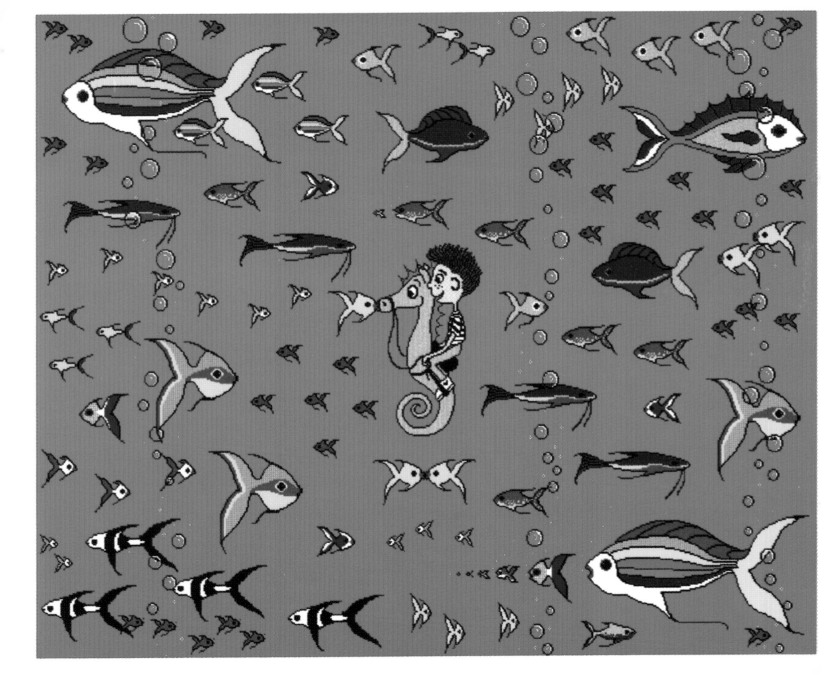

And perhaps a mean, old sea witch -
she won't catch you, but she'll try!

Now you're finally back home again,
and going out to play . . .

But you might just meet a seahorse,
on a *very* lucky day.

And if he wore a saddle,
and were tied up to a tree . . .

He'd be very glad to see you,
for he'd know *you'd* set him free!